W9-BUR-612

E
G868d

Copyright © 1991 by Susanna Gretz   All rights reserved. No part of this book may be reproduced or transmitted in any form or by any means, electronic or mechanical, including photocopying, recording, or by any information storage and retrieval system, without permission in writing from the Publisher.   Four Winds Press, Macmillan Publishing Company, 866 Third Avenue, New York, NY 10022.   Collier Macmillan Canada, Inc., 1200 Eglinton Avenue East, Suite 200, Don Mills, Ontario M3C 3N1.   First published in Great Britain in 1991 by Methuen Children's Books, London.   First American edition 1991.

Printed in Italy   10 9 8 7 6 5 4 3 2 1

Library of Congress Cataloging-in-Publication Data Gretz, Susanna. Duck takes off / Susanna Gretz. — 1st American ed.   p.   cm. Summary: Duck, Rabbit, and Frog have trouble playing school when each possesses such different skills from the other. ISBN 0-02-737472-6 [1. Animals – Fiction. 2. Friendship – Fiction. 3. Play – Fiction.] I. Title. PZ7.G8636Du 1991 [E] – dc20 90-3846 CIP AC

+
E
G868d

Duck Takes Off

Susanna Gretz

Four Winds Press
New York

RETA E. KING LIBRARY
CHADRON STATE COLLEGE
CHADRON, NE 69337

Duck loves to show off.
"I'll be the teacher," she says,
"and you're the schoolchildren."

"Yes, Miss," says Rabbit.
"Yes, Miss," says Frog.

"First you have to learn *diving*," says Duck.
"Just watch me, I'm a great diver!"

Frog is good at diving.

Rabbit isn't.
"I'm a land animal, Miss," he says.
"I can't do that."

"You *have* to, I'm the teacher," says Duck.
Rabbit tries.

"Now you have to learn *quacking*," says Duck.
But Frog isn't very good at quacking.

Neither is Rabbit.
"I can't do that, Miss," he says.

"You *have* to, I'm the teacher,"
says Duck.
"I'm not your friend anymore,"
says Rabbit.

"Well then, *you'll* have to learn *waddling*,"
Duck tells Frog. But Frog isn't any good at waddling.

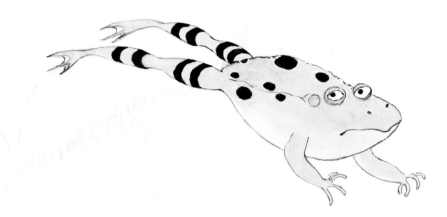

"I can't do that, Miss," she says.

"You *have* to!" says Duck. Frog tries again.

"NO!" yells Duck. "That's all wrong."

"I'm not your friend anymore," says Frog.

Now Duck is all alone.
"I'll play school by myself," she says.

But this isn't any fun.

Then she rounds up her toys.
"I'm the teacher," she tells them.

This isn't fun either.

Frog is all alone, too.

So is Rabbit.
"Maybe I'll take a walk,"
he says to himself.

RETA E. KING LIBRARY
CHADRON STATE COLLEGE
CHADRON, NE 69337

Duck is also out walking.
"Hello, Miss Bossy," says Rabbit.
"I'm not bossy anymore," says Duck.

And then they meet Frog.
"Hello, Miss Show-off," says Frog.
"I won't show off anymore," says Duck.
"Let's play school again . . . and Rabbit can be teacher first."
"Hmmm," says Frog.

First Rabbit teaches them digging.
Frog can only dig backwards.

"Backwards is all right," says Rabbit.

"Duck is digging with her beak!" says Frog.
"That's all right, too," says Rabbit.

Next Frog teaches hopping.
"I already know how to hop," says Rabbit.
He helps Frog teach Duck. "Good," he says.
"You've nearly got it, Duck," says Frog.

And then it's Duck's turn to be the teacher.
"What are we going to learn, Miss?" asks Rabbit.
"Tell us, Miss," says Frog.
"Let's see," says Duck, "you have to learn. . .

FLYING!"
"But --" says Rabbit.
"No buts," says Duck.
"Just watch me!"

Duck takes off.

"Duck has forgotten all about us," says Rabbit.
"Let's play hopscotch instead."

"Or leapfrog," says Frog. So they did.